BIG MEN, BIG COUNTRY

BIG MEN, BIG COUNTRY

A COLLECTION OF AMERICAN TALL TALES

WRITTEN BY

Paul Robert Walker

ILLUSTRATED BY

James Bernardin

Harcourt Brace Jovanovich, Publishers

San Diego   New York   London

HBJ

Requests for permission to make copies
of any part of the work should be mailed to:
Permissions Department,
Harcourt Brace Jovanovich, Publishers, 8th Floor,
Orlando, Florida 32887.

Library of Congress Cataloging-in-Publication Data
Walker, Paul Robert.
Big men, big country/by Paul Robert Walker; illustrated by
James Bernardin.
p.   cm.
Includes bibliographical references.
Summary: A collection of American tall tales featuring such
legendary characters as Davy Crockett, Paul Bunyan, and Pecos Bill.
ISBN 0-15-207136-9
1. Tales—United States.   2. Tall tales—United States.   [1. Tall
tales. 2. Folklore—United States.]   I. Bernardin, James, ill.
II. Title.
PZ8.1.W1287Bi   1993
398.21′0973   91-45126

First edition
A B C D E

M5354

To my brother Brian,
a walking, talking tall tale
—P. R. W.

To my parents
and Lisa
—J. B.

Contents

Author's Note

AMERICA IS A BIG COUNTRY—a great whopper of a land from sea to sea, across tall mountains, wide prairies, and endless deserts. In its early years, it was a country made for heroes—a new land where big men faced big challenges and overcame them in amazing ways. Tall tales existed long before the first pioneers came to America, but it was in America that the tall tale found its natural home.

Life on the American frontier was mostly back-breaking work. But when the work was done, folks gathered around the fire and created their own entertainment. Storytelling was an art, and they would sit for hours telling tales of the new land. The rugged folks of the American frontier weren't much interested in repeating a tale the same way they heard it. They wanted to make the story bigger and better.

If Jack told how he shot a deer and a bear with one bullet, Tom said that was pretty fine shooting, but *he* shot a deer, a bear, *and* a fish with one bullet. Then Frank allowed how those were both pretty good shots, but he also shot a deer, a bear, and a fish with one bullet—and when he cut the fish open, there was a gold ring inside! Frank didn't expect Jack and Tom to believe his tall tale, but he enjoyed telling it—and they enjoyed listening.

At first, the hero of the tale was often the fellow who told it, or maybe it was a "fella down the road." But as a story was passed from campfire to campfire and from cabin to cabin, it just didn't seem right that such a wonderful tale should be told about an ordinary man. Pretty soon, folks decided that the story really happened to a more famous hero—a rip-roarin' character who lived for great adventures.

Some were real heroes, like Davy Crockett and Jim Bridger; others were made-up heroes, like Paul Bunyan and Pecos Bill; others were just great storytellers, like John Darling and Gib Morgan. Sometimes, the same story was told about several heroes: John Darling, Paul Bunyan, and Pecos Bill all had similar adventures with giant mosquitoes; Old Stormalong's ship, Gib Morgan's oil derrick, and Pecos Bill's wife all got in the way of the moon.

The heroes of American tall tales did not always act the way we believe our heroes should act today. They smoked, drank, cussed, and got downright violent with animals, Indians, and each other. We no longer respect these qualities, but they reflect the values of the American frontier. People in those days felt that it took big, tough men to tame a big, tough country.

But what about big, tough women? There were plenty of strong women on the American frontier. In fact, women did most of the civilizing while the men ran around and got into trouble. But the only major female characters in American tall tales are Davy Crockett's wife, Sally Ann Thunder Crockett, and Pecos Bill's wife, Slue-Foot

Sue. You see, in those days most folks believed that a woman's place was beside her husband. Of course, today we know that it's the other way around.

Let's face it, these American heroes were a little rough on the outside. But they were fine folks where it counts the most—in the heart and mind and spirit. A tall tale hero helped his friends and neighbors, solved his problems in imaginative ways, and created a better world. These are American qualities that should never change.

All of the stories in this book are based on tall tales that were told by Americans in the nineteenth and early twentieth centuries. Some tales began orally—around a campfire, in a log cabin, or even on a city street corner. Others began with the written word, in a book or popular magazine. After each of these stories, you will find a short factual section that provides more information about the tale and its source.

Most American tall tales—in their original versions—are not complete stories with beginnings, middles, and ends. Oral tales are usually brief anecdotes, like the bullet that brought down three animals and a gold ring. Written tales are usually collections of anecdotes about a particular hero. These are interesting and entertaining, but they are not always satisfying to a modern reader.

In researching this collection, I have gone back to the earliest available version of each tale. I have tried to be as true as possible to these original versions. But I have also added or changed a few details to connect the shorter anecdotes, establish the plot, and create more lively characters. In the great tradition of American storytelling, I have not simply repeated the stories—I have tried to make them bigger and better.

—P. R. W.

BIG MEN, BIG COUNTRY

Davy Crockett Teaches the Steamboat a Leetle Patriotism

BACK IN THE EARLY DAYS of our country, when pioneers were settling the wilderness between the Appalachian Mountains and the Mississippi River, there was a half-horse, half-alligator, half–snapping turtle kind of man called a ring-tailed roarer. The ring-tailed roarers were bigger, stronger, and smarter than the average pioneer. They could shoot straighter, fight harder, and yell louder. And the biggest, strongest, smartest, straight-shootingest, hard-fightingest, loud-yellingest ring-tailed roarer of the whole bunch was Davy Crockett.

Davy lived in a log cabin deep in the wilderness of Tennessee. There weren't many human folks in the neighborhood, but that was just fine with Davy because there were plenty of bears, panthers, wildcats, critters, and varmints. Davy's best friend was a bear named Death Hug. While Davy smoked his big bowl pipe in one corner of the cabin, Death Hug smoked his small bowl pipe in the other corner.

Davy was usually a pretty happy ring-tailed roarer, but one morning he woke up in a terrible mood. "Death Hug," he growled, "I am feeling so wolfish and cantankerous that I could swallow a rattlesnake and spit out the rattles. What say we wander over to the Big Muddy and ride on one of them locomotive river towns they call a steamboat?"

Of course, Death Hug knew that the Big Muddy was the Mississippi River. He didn't know much about steamboats, but he was willing to go along if it would make Davy feel better. So he packed his small bowl pipe and opened the door of the cabin. Davy packed his big bowl pipe, put on his coonskin cap, and shouldered his old splendiferous rifle, Brown Betty. Then they set out for the Big Muddy.

After a long morning's walk through the forest, Davy was feeling a mite less wolfish and cantankerous. When they reached the Big Muddy, he and Death Hug stood on the bank and gazed out over the broad, rolling river. They saw no sign of the steamboat, but there was plenty of river.

"I think I'll take a leetle nap," said Davy. He tied a fishing line around his big toe and tied the other end around a tree. Then he walked right out into the river and lay down on top of the water. Death Hug curled up on the bank.

Davy was snoozing and floating on the Big Muddy when he felt a sharp poke in his ribs. He woke to see what kind of wild critter was trying to take a bite out of him, but the critter looked almost human. He wore a big round hat with a long ribbon in the back and white cloth trousers that were so wide it looked like he was about to sail away. The humanish critter stood on a raft made of three kegs fastened to a log, and he held a long pole—which he was using to poke Davy in the ribs.

"Stranger," said Davy, "by the looks of your face you must be human, but you are one of the greatest curiosities I've ever seen in these parts."

"By the devil," said the stranger, "the thing speaks just like a human being! I thought I had poked a catfish."

"You infernal heathen!" cried Davy. "I'm a ring-tailed roarer! I can run faster, jump higher, dive deeper, stay under longer, and come up drier than any man in the country. If you don't float along and let me finish my nap, I'll chew you up like a snapping turtle and rub you down like an alligator."

The stranger's face turned red as a shovelful of hot coals. "You freshwater lubber!" he roared. "You rock crab! You deck swabber!"

Davy stood up on the water and looked the stranger in the eye. He was getting wolfish and cantankerous all over again. "My name's Crockett!" he roared back. "I'll put my mark on your infernal wolf hide before you've gone the length of a panther's tail!"

The stranger's face returned to its normal color. "Crockett?" he asked. "Davy Crockett?"

"The same," said Davy.

"Well, why didn't you say so, old chap? My name's Ben Hardin, and I've sailed fourteen times around the world. Let's shake our flippers and be done with it." Ben stretched his hand out toward Davy, and Davy stretched his hand out toward Ben. Then they shook hands and felt totalaciously better.

"Ben," said Davy, "I'm going on a steamboat ride with my bear, Death Hug. You bein' a sailor an' all, maybe you'd like to join us."

"I'd be honored, old chap," said Ben.

The two men floated to shore, where Davy introduced Ben to Death Hug. Ben shook Death Hug's paw and said, "A friend of Davy

Crockett is a friend of Ben Hardin." Death Hug grinned and puffed on his small bowl pipe.

A few minutes later, the steamboat arrived. It was even bigger and more splendiferous than Davy had expected. It had three decks, two tall smokestacks, and a paddle wheel the size of Davy's log cabin.

"Creation!" Davy exclaimed. "That locomotive river town carries more folks than the state of Tennessee! C'mon, boys, let's see how she rides."

Davy, Ben, and Death Hug strolled up the gangplank and waited to buy their tickets. There were folks getting on and folks getting off and trunks and cargo being loaded and unloaded—it was as busy and colorful as a day at the circus! But when they got to the front of the line, the captain shook his head and closed the gate. "No bears allowed," he said.

"You panther pup!" Davy cried. "My bear travels where I travel."

"I'm sorry, sir," said the captain politely. "It's company policy."

"I'll chew your unpatriotic policy and spit it out for wildcat meat!" Davy roared. "Maybe you ain't heard that this here is the United States of America, where every citizen, human or bearlike, has the right to ride in a steamboat."

The captain's face turned crimson and his voice got a mite less polite. "Maybe you ain't heard that this is the finest steamboat on the Big Muddy," he said. "She can pass any boat on the water and leave it behind like a tree on the shore."

"Well, I'm Davy Crockett," Davy bellowed, "the darling son of Tennessee. I can eat up a rattlesnake, hold a buffalo out to drink, and shoot a rifle ball through the moon."

"I don't care who you are," snarled the captain. "A policy is a policy, and a bear is a bear. No bears allowed."

Now Davy was feelin' wolfish and cantankerous for the third time in one day. "C'mon, boys," he said, "let's teach this steamboat a leetle patriotism."

With Ben and Death Hug following, Davy stormed down the gangplank and into the forest. He found a hollow gum tree and chopped it down with a flash of lightning from his eyes. Then he hacked it open on one side, so it looked like a long, narrow canoe. Ben Hardin corked it inside and out to make it watertight, and Death Hug cut a pair of ten-foot paddles with his powerful claws. The three friends launched the tree onto the Big Muddy just as the big steamboat was disappearing from view.

Davy and Ben lit their big bowl pipes and paddled in the bow, blowing smoke just like a steam engine. Death Hug lit his small bowl pipe and stood in the stern, steering with his stump of a tail and

19

holding up the American flag. Things went a little slow at first, but the pipes kept smoking, Davy and Ben kept paddling, and Death Hug kept steering. Pretty soon, the fish were staring in wonder, and the banks of the Big Muddy were flying by so fast it looked like one big blur of river, trees, and sky. Before you could say "ring-tailed roarer" the hollow gum tree passed that unpatriotic steamboat in sassy, splendiferous triumph.

"Ahoy, matey!" cried Ben Hardin, shaking his big bowl pipe at the captain of the steamboat.

Death Hug grinned and waved the American flag.

Davy Crockett stood in the hollow gum tree and doffed his coonskin cap to the Stars and Stripes. "Well, boys," he said, "I guess we taught that locomotive river town a leetle bit of patriotism. There's nothin' a steamboat can do that American brains and brawn—human or bearlike—can't do better. It makes me so downright proud I've gotta tell the whole Big Muddy."

Setting his cap on his head, Davy clapped his arms to his sides like a rooster. "Cock-a-doodle-doo!" he crowed. "Who-who-whoop! Bow-wow-wow for the United States of America!" Then he lifted Brown Betty to his shoulder, aimed at the sky, and shot a rifle ball right through the middle of the moon.

Davy Crockett was born in eastern Tennessee in 1786. During his adult life, he made a series of westward moves across the state, each time venturing farther into the wilderness. In 1827, he was elected to represent western Tennessee in the U.S. House of Representatives. His humorous speeches and plain good sense made him famous as a symbol of the country's uneducated but intelligent backwoodsmen.

In his speeches, Crockett often turned his real-life experiences into tall tales about hunting, Indian fighting, and other frontier activities. Many of these stories were recorded in two books, Sketches and Eccentricities of Col. David Crockett, of West Tennessee *(1833), written anonymously, and* A Narrative of the Life of David Crockett *(1834), written by Crockett with Thomas Chilton. These books, along with his speeches, made Davy Crockett a legend during his lifetime.*

In 1835, a new kind of book called the Crockett Almanac *appeared. It was an inexpensive publication similar to a magazine, and it included stories about Davy Crockett as well as other tales and information about the frontier. The* Crockett Almanac *was very popular, and new editions were published regularly until 1856. Although the almanacs were written anonymously, it is possible that Crockett had a hand in writing the early editions.*

After Crockett's death in 1836—while fighting at the Alamo in the Texas Revolution—the stories in the Crockett Almanacs *became wilder and wilder. Soon the real Davy Crockett was replaced by Davy Crockett the tall tale hero. This tall tale is based on three separate anecdotes from the* Crockett Almanacs.

Old Stormalong
Finds a Man-Sized Ship

OLD STORMALONG WAS THE GREATEST sailor who ever sailed the seas. He stood four fathoms high, drank his soup from a Cape Cod dory, and ate a shark for dinner with ostrich eggs on the side. When he was finished, he stretched out on the deck and picked his teeth with an eighteen-foot oar.

Now, a fathom is the height of a good-sized man and a dory is a fair-sized rowboat. So Old Stormalong, well, he was a mighty big sailor. He had a hard time fitting on an ordinary ship, so he went from ship to ship, just trying to get comfortable. Finally he ended up as boatswain on the *Lady of the Sea*, the biggest ship in the Atlantic—at least that's what Stormy thought.

After a long voyage through the Caribbean, the *Lady* was heading for her home port of Boston. As she neared the Jersey coast, just off Barnegat Light, the weather turned bad, and the *Lady*—big as she was—tossed like a toy on the huge waves.

As Stormy peered through the growing tempest, he caught sight of something totally unexpected. A great new city was floating calm as could be on the stormy sea.

"It's unnatural!" he exclaimed. "How could the landlubbers build a city on the sea?" But as the *Lady* drew closer, he realized it wasn't a city at all. It was a ship! The biggest ship he'd ever seen—it made the *Lady of the Sea* look like a rowboat! Even from a distance he could read the name painted on the huge bow in letters twenty feet high: *Courser*.

Stormy leaned over the rail and gazed in admiration. "Now, that's a ship," he said with a sigh. "Aye, a man could stretch his legs on a ship like that."

Without bothering to take his gear from below, Stormy jumped over the side and swam toward the *Courser*. The seas were rough, but his powerful strokes brought him alongside the huge ship in a few minutes. He called for a rope and pulled himself aboard.

"And who might you be?" asked the captain.

"Alfred Bulltop Stormalong," Stormy replied. "At your service, sir."

"Well, sign the log," said the captain. "We can use a big man like you."

Stormy took a look around. The first thing he noticed was the horses—a whole stableful right on the deck!

"She's a horseboat, is she?" asked Stormy.

The captain laughed and patted Stormy on the back of the knee. "Horseboat, my eye!" he said. "Those are for the men on watch. The deck's so big, they have to ride around it."

Stormy smiled and took a deep breath of the tangy salt air. "Aye," he said. "She's the ship for me."

And so she was. The *Courser* carried over six hundred men to keep her running trim. A man had to get out his compass to find his way from fore to aft. The sails were so big that they had to be made in the Sahara Desert—just to give the sailmakers room to spread them out. Bunkhouses and galleys were built up and down the masts, and the crow's nest was lost in the clouds. If a young man climbed the rigging, he was an old man by the time he came down.

Until Stormy came aboard, it took thirty-two men just to turn the wheel. But Old Stormalong could handle it steady by himself. Oh, he was a sight to see! A strong, handsome, four-fathom man in a peacoat as big as an ordinary sail. His black beard speckled with spray; his huge hands wrapped around the steering pegs; his dark eyes fixed on the horizon. Stormy was the only man aboard who could actually see where the ship was going.

The *Courser* could ride through an average storm as if she were floating on a millpond. In fact, during all the years that Old Stormalong handled the wheel, only two storms ever blew her off course.

The first was a September gale in the North Atlantic. The wind blew and blew like the devil himself—whipping the huge sails and spraying cold salt water across the decks until it was hard to tell whether a man was on the ship or in the sea. The fog was so thick that Stormy couldn't see the end of his beard. But he held the great wheel for two weeks straight—day and night—without eating or sleeping.

Finally, the winds died down and the fog lifted. When the sun rose over the cold blue water, the navigator discovered that they had been blown into the North Sea, and they were heading south—straight for disaster. You see, the *Courser* was much too big to turn around and a mite too big to pass through the English Channel.

Old Stormalong held the wheel steady while the officers rode around the deck shouting orders and watching the sides of the ship. As the *Courser* approached the narrowest point of the Channel— between Calais and the cliffs of Dover—the captain ordered the sails reefed and the men into the lifeboats.

"Hold fast!" shouted Stormy. "I think we can make it, sir."

"Are you sure?" asked the captain.

"It'll be close," said Stormy. "But if ye send all hands over and lay a coat of soap on the sides, we just might squeeze through. Better coat it extra heavy on the starboard—those Dover cliffs look mighty rough."

The captain ordered the crew to coat the sides as thick and slippery as they could. When the ship hit the bottleneck, she *just* squeezed through—it was so tight that the soap on the starboard side rubbed off against the cliffs. It's still there today, and that's why they're called the White Cliffs of Dover.

Two Septembers later, the *Courser* was sailing through the Caribbean Sea when a hurricane blew out of the northeast with a force that made that North Sea gale look like a gentle breeze. The captain wasn't worried about the ship—there wasn't a storm in the world that could break the *Courser*. But he was afraid the great vessel would run into an island, harming the people, their homes, and their towns.

"Mister Stormalong!" the captain cried. "Steer clear of the islands and hold her steady as she goes!"

Old Stormalong clenched the great wheel, his knuckles white as the sails, and steered the great ship past Puerto Rico, Hispaniola, and Jamaica. But the storm had a will of its own, and it drove the *Courser* straight toward the isthmus of Panama. In those days, the isthmus was solid land, separating the Atlantic Ocean on one side from the Pacific Ocean on the other side. It was wild, unpopulated jungle.

There was nothing Stormy could do—the mighty ship hit the land, sailed right through the isthmus, and emerged in the Pacific Ocean. The *Courser* didn't show a scratch, but she'd dug a deep ditch across the isthmus. Some folks call it the Panama Canal.

As the years passed, Stormy's beard grew white and his eyes looked beyond the horizon. One fine morning, he steered the *Courser* into deep blue water, where no danger lurked within a hundred miles. He took one last look at the sea, and he drew one last breath of the fine sea air. Then he closed his eyes and leaned forward on the wheel. Old Stormalong was gone.

When they reached port, the men of the *Courser* buried Stormy by the shore, so he would always feel the salt spray of the sea. As they said good-bye to the greatest sailor of them all, they sang this song:

Old Stormy's dead and gone to rest,
To my way hey, Stormalong, John!
Of all the sailors he was the best,
To my aye, aye, aye, aye, Mister Stormalong!

The lyrics at the end of this tall tale are taken from a sailor's song called "Stormalong." This type of song is called a chantey, and it was sung by sailors as they worked on the great wooden ships of the nineteenth century. No one knows where the song came from or if there really was a sailor called Old Stormalong. But to the men of the sea, he was a symbol of the strength and bravery of a great sailor.

This tall tale is based on anecdotes recorded by Frank Shay in Here's Audacity! American Legendary Folk Heroes. *Although the "Stormalong" song is an authentic nineteenth-century song of the sea, there are different opinions as to the authenticity of the anecdotes. One obvious conflict is that Stormy—the symbol of wooden ships and the early nineteenth-century sailor—is supposed to have dug the Panama Canal, which was completed in 1914. This indicates that the anecdotes were created much later than the song, but it makes the tall tale even taller.*

Big Mose
and the Lady Washington

BIG MOSE WAS THE BRAVEST fireman in the city of New York—in fact, he was the bravest fireman in all of America. He was always the first to do his duty, and he loved the machine like he loved his own mother. The "machine" was the fire engine—the old gal— Lady Washington Engine No. 40.

In Mose's time, fire engines were different than they are today. They looked like big wagons, with a shiny condenser in the middle and long poles, called brakes, on the sides. The brakes were like giant pump handles, and it took ten or twenty men on each brake to pump the water through the condenser into the hose and right smack dab into the middle of the flames. It took fifty or even a hundred men to pull the heavy engine to the fire.

Mose was a little different, too. He stood eight feet tall, and his high-crowned beaver hat stood two feet taller. A flaming shock of orange hair covered the back of his head, and his thick side-whiskers

were plastered down with the finest bear grease. His huge hands hung to his knees like two Virginia hams. He wore a red flannel shirt, striped suspenders with a leather double-eagle on the back, and blue-black pants folded above giant boots with copper-plated soles.

Sykesy was Mose's best friend and sidekick. He was just an average-sized teenage boy, so he came up to Mose's belt—even wearing his little plug hat. Like the rest of the boys, Sykesy ran alongside the machine and helped out wherever help was needed. His greatest dream was to be a full-fledged fireman just like Mose.

When they weren't fighting fires, Mose and Sykesy liked nothing better than to strut along the Bowery, the finest, glitteriest street in New York. There were theaters, restaurants, hotels, stores, parks, and gardens. Why, some of the buildings were five stories high!

One day Mose and Sykesy were strolling down the wide avenue, taking in the sights and sounds. "Sykesy, my boy," said Mose, "'tis a gallus day if ever I seen one."

"It ain't nothin' else," agreed Sykesy, trying to keep pace with Mose's huge strides.

Mose and Sykesy had a funny way of talking, but they always knew what they meant. "Gallus" meant "great, grand, and beautiful," all at the same time. "It ain't nothin' else" was just a polite way of saying "Yes."

Just then a streetcar rolled up the Bowery, drawn by two dapple-gray horses. A huge grin spread over Mose's face and his eyes twinkled with mischief. He took two big strides into the center of the street and hoisted the streetcar onto his shoulder, with the horses dangling from their traces.

"Let us down!" cried the passengers.

"Please, Mose!" begged the driver.

"Don't worry yer heads," said Mose pleasantly. "I'll get you there in half the time." With Sykesy trotting behind, Mose continued striding up the Bowery, carrying the streetcar and laughing with joy. His laugh was so deep and strong that it blew the leaves off the trees and echoed like the rushing roar of Niagara Falls.

As Mose and the streetcar approached the corner of Broome Street, a fire alarm sounded throughout the East Side. The church bells rang and the call passed up and down the Bowery: "Fire on Essex! Fire on Essex!" Without even stopping to think, Sykesy ran toward the headquarters of Lady Washington Engine Company No. 40. "Ain't you coming, Mose?" he called.

"Don't I do my duty?" Mose asked. But it wasn't really a question, because Mose always did his duty. He set the streetcar lightly onto the street, patted the horses on their heads, and ran off toward the firehouse.

By the time Mose and Sykesy arrived, the other firemen were already pulling the old gal out of the garage. There were fifty men at the ropes and two hundred boys running beside her. Sykesy took Mose's tall beaver hat and handed him his giant fire helmet. Then Mose took his place among the men, Sykesy joined the boys, and off they ran toward the fire.

As he pulled on the rope, Mose glanced back at the beautiful old gal. She was a gallus engine—the finest in the city. Her brakes were plated silver, her pipes were new, and there was a picture of Martha Washington—the mother of our country—as big as life on the back of the condenser. It made Mose's heart proud to be a member of Lady Washington Engine Company No. 40.

They were running down the middle of the Bowery now, heading straight for the fire. It looked like a bad one—Mose could see black smoke billowing over the rooftops. Suddenly another engine turned onto the Bowery and blocked the path of Lady Washington. Mose scowled in anger. It was Black Joke Engine No. 33! She had a hundred men at the ropes and three hundred boys running beside her. With the extra manpower, she was sure to get to the fire first and win the glory.

"Whatcha gonna do?" cried Sykesy, running beside Mose. "That Black Joke engine always tries to beat us to the fire."

"Run ahead and get the plug, Sykesy," ordered Mose. "Black Joke won't beat the old gal today."

As Sykesy disappeared down the street, Mose bellowed in a voice that shook the buildings. "Hand me the ropes, hosses! I'm taking the reins meself." The other firemen dropped away. Mose slung the long ropes over his broad shoulders and ran through the heart of the Bowery, pulling Lady Washington as if she were a one-horse cart. The hundred men at the ropes of Black Joke Engine No. 33 stared in wide-eyed wonder as the old gal passed them by with a single man at the ropes and the rest of the company running behind.

When Mose and the engine arrived at the burning building, Sykesy was sitting casually on a barrel. Mose pulled the engine up to the barrel, and Sykesy jumped off to reveal the most convenient fire hydrant on the whole street. "Good work, Sykesy," said Mose, connecting the hose to the hydrant. "All right, hosses, man the brakes!"

The firemen worked the brakes, pumping up and down with all their strength to send the water high into the flames. Mose took the end of the hose and stepped right up to the red-hot building, aiming the stream of water with an expert's eye. It was a bad fire, and they would need all the help they could get—including Black Joke Engine No. 33. But Lady Washington was a gallus old gal, and she deserved the glory for being first.

As the other engine companies arrived, a young woman rushed toward Mose, crying hysterically, "My babies! My poor babies!"

"What's the matter, good woman?" asked Mose.

"My three children are still in the building," she wailed, pointing at the highest window. "There—on the fifth floor."

Mose squinted up into the smoke. The flames were licking at the woodwork, and it looked like the whole floor was about to go. He motioned to Sykesy and handed him the end of the hose. "Sykesy, take the nozzle," he ordered. "I'm going in."

Sykesy proudly took the end of the hose and pointed it toward the heart of the fire. He was a real fireman now.

Mose grabbed the longest ladder he could find and leaned it against the burning building. It only reached to the second floor, but Mose climbed it anyway, up through the flames and the red-hot embers. At the top of the ladder he balanced on the last rung, stretched all eight feet of his body, and reached with his long arms upward toward the third-floor window. With the strength of his powerful fingers he pulled himself up and stood on the burning windowsill. He stretched toward the fourth floor and pulled himself up again. Finally he reached the fifth-floor window and disappeared into the flames.

Moments later, Big Mose reappeared at the window carrying three children. A little boy rode the fireman's back, his arms wrapped around Mose's thick neck. A little girl was curled in Mose's huge right arm. And with his left arm, Mose held a tiny bundle securely against his chest.

"The ladder ain't no use for going down," Mose told the children. "Hold on tight, little people!" Without a moment's hesitation, Big Mose jumped from the flame-licked window and landed with a solid thud on the ground, five floors below.

"Here you are, good woman," he said, handing the children to their mother.

"Oh, how can I ever repay you?" the woman asked.

"Don't you worry about that," said Mose, doffing his huge fireman's helmet. "Just keep these babies safe, and when they get all growed up, you can tell them about a gallus old gal called Lady Washington Engine No. 40."

Mose strolled over to Sykesy and reached for the end of the hose. "Are you all right?" asked Sykesy.

Mose took the nozzle and smiled. "I ain't nothin' else."

In 1848 a play called A Glance at New York *became the hit of the theater season. The hero of the play was Mose, a volunteer fireman who had a funny way of talking, rough manners, and a heart of gold.* A Glance at New York *was performed throughout the country, and other Mose plays and Mose almanacs—similar to the* Crockett Almanacs*—were produced during the next decade.*

Mose was based on a real volunteer fireman named Moses Humphrey, who was also the leader of a gang called the Bowery Boys. During the later nineteenth century, the real Moses Humphrey and the character of Mose became combined into a tall tale hero called Big Mose, who was so big and strong that he could carry streetcars and swim the Hudson River in two strokes. This tall tale is based on A Glance at New York, *by Benjamin A. Baker, and two books by Herbert Asbury:* The Gangs of New York *and* Ye Olde Fire Laddies.

John Darling and the Skeeter Chariot

THE CATSKILL MOUNTAINS OF New York State are mighty beautiful. The air is lavender-pink and the moon floats in the sky like a friendly ship. But even with pink air and a friendly moon, the Catskills are a bad place to be a farmer. The ground is rocky and the winters are long and cold.

John Darling was just a little man—not much bigger than a boy—with sandy hair, a smiling face, and pale blue eyes that twinkled with mischief. He tried to be a good farmer, but as he walked behind the plow, he dreamed of distant lands and great riches.

One day, John was plowing the rocky soil of his Catskill Mountain farm, dreaming of golden nuggets. He had seven oxen yoked to the plow, and the sharp blade was cutting deep into the hard ground. Suddenly a rabbit ran across their path. The great beasts started with fright and stampeded, dragging John and the plow after them.

John desperately steered the plow toward a giant oak stump,

hoping to stop the frightened beasts. But the oxen pulled the plow—and little John Darling—right through the heart of the stump. As John came out on the other side, the stump closed up and caught him by the seat of the pants. The plow handles broke off and the seven oxen kept running, leaving John stuck in the stump with the broken plow handles still in his hands.

John struggled to get free, but that old oak stump wasn't about to let go. So he tossed the broken plow handles on the rocky ground, climbed out of his pants, and stood in the middle of the field, dressed in nothing but his long underwear.

"Tarnation!" he cried. "I'm through with this rocky ground and these man-eating stumps. They've discovered gold in California, and I aim to find some."

John Darling left the Catskill Mountains and headed for the gold fields of California. It was a long, hard trip across the wilderness. He didn't have much money to start with, and by the time he reached California—well, there wasn't a penny in his pockets. Gold-mining supplies cost money, so John took a job as a sugarbush man.

A sugarbush is a big green bush that's just dripping with sugary sap. A sugarbush man picks the bushes, loads them into a 56-pound pan, and boils them down for their sugar. It was hard work, but John was a Catskill farmer and hard work was nothing new to him. He turned out to be the best sugarbush man in all of California.

John had almost saved enough money to head for the gold fields when one day a huge black cloud appeared in the sky.

"B'gor," said John. "Looks like rain."

But as the cloud got closer he saw that it wasn't rain at all. It was mosquitoes—the biggest mosquitoes he had ever seen. They were carrying cows and pigs and horses, and it looked like they wanted a sandy-haired little sugarbush man. John dove under his 56-pound pan and waited for the attack.

"Bing! Bing! Bing!" The huge mosquitoes drove their stingers through the metal pan. Crouching inside, John dodged their long sharp tips. Pretty soon there were two dozen stingers sticking through the pan, lined up in two neat rows. Suddenly John Darling had a great vision in that dreamy brain of his.

He reached up and grabbed one stinger from each row; then he tied them together with a good strong sailor's knot. The mosquitoes buzzed and beat on the sugarbush pan, but the knot held tight. John tied another pair of stingers and another and another until all two dozen were tied into half-hoops. Then he climbed inside and lay down, just like in a hammock. It was nice and comfortable, but the giant mosquitoes didn't like it a bit. They buzzed and beat their wings until they lifted the 56-pound sugarbush pan off the ground—and John Darling along with it. He was flying!

"Head south, skeeters," he ordered. "I've always wanted to see South America."

Well, the mosquitoes were mighty angry, so they flew in the wrong direction. They took John out over the Pacific Ocean and on across the blue water for many days until they finally landed in a beautiful garden. By then the mosquitoes were worn out, so they just buzzed quietly while John climbed out of the sugarbush pan and stretched his legs.

"Land o'Goshen!" he exclaimed, looking around the garden. " 'Tis the most beautiful place I've ever seen."

A dark-haired woman in a golden kimono approached him and bowed. "Welcome," she said.

"Thank you," said John. "Is this South America?"

The woman laughed, holding a delicate lavender fan to her face. "No," she said. "This is China, and I am the queen."

John smiled and bowed deeply. "I am John Darling of the Catskill Mountains in New York State," he said.

"We are honored by your visit, John Darling," said the queen. "The people of China would like to give you a special gift." As the queen walked toward the other side of the garden, John wondered what the gift would be. Gold? Silver? Jewels?

The queen of China returned and handed John Darling a young piglet. "This piglet was born on my royal farm," said the queen. "It will grow up to be a fine pig."

At first John was disappointed, but as he took the wriggling creature in his arms he realized that it was just about the prettiest little piglet he had ever seen. "Thank you, Your Majesty," he said. "I'm a farmer myself, and I know a fine piglet when I see one."

For the first time since he left for California, John Darling felt homesick for his farm in the Catskill Mountains. To a real farmer, a pretty pink piglet is worth more than all the gold in the world. So John said good-bye to the queen of China and climbed back into the 56-pound sugarbush pan, holding the squirming piglet under his shirt. "Home, skeeters!" he ordered.

The giant mosquitoes weren't angry anymore, so they flew straight over the Pacific Ocean, over California and the big country, and landed right on John's farm in the Catskill Mountains of New York State.

John climbed out of the sugarbush pan and untied the mosquitoes' stingers. "There's some nice pickin's down in the Jersey swamps," he told them. "Grow fat and live long."

John watched the giant mosquitoes fly away. Then he carried the piglet across the field toward the big oak stump. His pants were still stuck in the stump, and the broken plow handles were still on the rocky ground. John Darling laughed and squeezed the pretty piglet. The air was lavender-pink, and the moon was rising like a friendly ship. It was good to be home.

John Darling was born in 1809 in the Catskill Mountains of New York. During his lifetime he became famous throughout the Catskills as a teller of humorous tales based on his experiences in farming and other frontier activities, including a trip to the California gold fields. Darling also told stories about places he had never been, like his visit with the queen of China—which sounds more like a visit to Japan.

After Darling's death in 1893, the people of the area continued to tell his stories. In the 1930s and 1940s, folklore experts wrote down the stories told by older people, who had heard them from John Darling himself when they were children. This tall tale is based on three stories reported by the people of the Catskills and recorded by Moritz Jagendorf in The Marvelous Adventures of Johnny Caesar Cicero Darling.

Ol' Gabe in the Valley of the Yellowstone

OL' GABE WAS RIDING THROUGH the valley of the upper Yellowstone, searching for some dinner. His hawk eyes missed nothing, from the snowcapped peaks in the distance to the twigs beneath his horse's feet. The hostiles were on the warpath, and it paid to be careful. Gabe had nothing personal against the Indians—after all, the land was theirs before the white man came. But he loved the land, too, and he wasn't leaving. He was a mountain man.

Ol' Gabe's rightful name was Jim Bridger, but all the trappers and fur traders called him Ol' Gabe 'cause he'd been in the mountains so gol'durned long. Why, some of them mountains were just little hills the first time he seen 'em. Now they were all growed up into big beautiful natural wonders.

Everywhere Gabe looked, there were amazing sights to see. Cliffs sparkling like diamonds. Hot geysers shooting up a hundred feet into

42

the air. Waterfalls cascading down into crystal pools. Those green-horns back East thought he was just telling stories 'bout the Yellow-stone. They called 'em "Jim Bridger's lies." Dagnabit! Ol' Gabe was as honest as the day is long—and he'd been visiting the Yellowstone for nigh on twenty years.

Out of the corner of his eye, Gabe spotted a big bull elk on the mountainside. It was a few hundred yards away—a mighty long shot, but just about in his range. He lifted his rifle, aimed, and squeezed the trigger. *Bam!* The sound of the shot echoed across the valley. As he brought the gun down, Ol' Gabe looked toward the elk, expecting to see the animal lying on the ground. But there it was, standing exactly where it stood before. It didn't even notice the shot!

Ol' Gabe felt a little embarrassed. After all, he had a reputation as a pretty fair shot, and that big bull elk was a good-sized target. Still, maybe it was farther away than it looked—distances can be deceptive in the Yellowstone. So Gabe reloaded his rifle and rode closer. He aimed extra careful, squeezed the trigger, and fired. *Bam!* The second shot echoed across the valley. Tarnation! That bull elk didn't even look up at the sound of the gun.

Ol' Gabe reloaded his rifle and rode so close that he could see the points on those big beautiful antlers. He raised his gun and aimed so careful, it was almost ridiculous. Then he fired. *Bam!*

Nothing. He reloaded and fired again. *Bam!*

Nothing. The cussed beast just stood there as pretty as a picture!

Now Ol' Gabe was getting steamed. He jumped off his horse and ran toward the elk, swinging his rifle over his head like a club. If the gol'durned animal didn't notice a ball and powder, maybe it'd pay attention to a good smack between the antlers.

Thump! Gabe crashed into an invisible wall and bounced backward onto the ground. He got up, shaking his head, and felt around. Why, it was a mountain of pure clear glass, separating him from the elk. No wonder the cussed creature didn't hear the shot!

He climbed back on his horse and rode around the glass mountain. All along the front of the mountain he could see that big bull elk just as clear as daylight. But when he got to the edge of the glass mountain the gol'durned beast turned into a tiny speck on a normal mountain about twenty-five miles away. That's when Ol' Gabe realized that the glass mountain was a natural telescope.

Well, there was no point in going after that elk. Gabe was mighty hungry now, so he continued on through the valley to Yellowstone Lake and camped beside his favorite fishing hole. What made this fishing hole so special was the boiling spring that flowed into the lake. For some reason—Ol' Gabe never could figure it out exactly—the hot water from the spring floated right on top of the cold water of the lake. This was pretty darn convenient for a hungry man. You see, all Gabe had to do was throw a line down into the cold water, catch a trout, and pull it back up through the hot water. By the time the trout got to the surface, it was all cooked and ready to eat.

The next morning—after a breakfast of boiled trout and beans—Ol' Gabe headed on across Peetrified Mountain. Back in the early days this particular mountain was cursed by an Indian medicine man. He was a pretty powerful medicine man, and now everything on the whole mountain was turned to stone. Some folks would call it petrified, but Ol' Gabe figured it was worse than that—it was downright *peetrified*.

The sagebrush, grass, and trees were all as peetrified as could be. The flowers were peetrified in bloom. The antelope, elk, bears, and other critters stood around like peetrified statues. The birds were peetrified in the sky, and their songs hung peetrified in the air. Why, even the sun and moon shone with peetrified light!

Ol' Gabe was working his way through this maze of peetrification when he caught the scent of Indian ponies—and it warn't no peetrified scent neither. He turned around, and sure enough there was a war party following him on the trail. As soon as they saw Gabe looking back, they whipped those ponies and galloped toward him like they meant business.

Now, Ol' Gabe was never one to run from a fight, but there were six of them and only one of him. So he figured the best thing was to skedaddle before he got peetrified, too. He whipped his horse and galloped across the mountain, speeding right past the peetrified elk and antelope and trees. The Indians were moving pretty fast themselves, and Gabe was riding just ahead of rifle range.

On the other side of the mountain there was a deep canyon—a couple hundred feet across and so far down it made you queasy just to look. Ol' Gabe pulled up to the edge and looked back at the Indians. They were coming fast and there wasn't much time for fancy tricks. He could either stand and face them or ride over the edge of the cliff. Either way, it looked like the end.

Then Ol' Gabe had an idea. He backed his horse a few steps up the trail, whipped it hard, and galloped right over the edge of the cliff. He kept on riding across the canyon and onto the other side. The Indians pulled up, startled, and stared across the canyon, wondering how in tarnation Ol' Gabe rode through the air. Gabe just waved and went on his way. He'd figured it right—you see, that mountain was so gol'durned peetrified that the law of gravity was peetrified, too.

Jim Bridger (1804–1881), nicknamed "Old Gabe," was one of the greatest mountain men, fur trappers, guides, and explorers in the history of the West. Around 1840 he visited the area that is now Yellowstone National Park. When he returned with stories of hot geysers and other natural wonders, people called them "Jim Bridger's lies." Frustrated with trying to tell a truth that no one believed, Bridger made up a series of tall tales in which he exaggerated the real natural wonders into even stranger marvels. The story of the elk and the glass mountain originated with a mass of volcanic glass called the Obsidian Cliff. The convenient fishing hole is only a slight exaggeration of the boiling pools around Yellowstone Lake. Peetrified Mountain is based on a petrified area called Specimen Ridge. These tall tales were recorded by Hiram Martin Chittenden in The Yellowstone National Park, *originally published in 1895.*

Paul Bunyan and
the Winter of the Blue Snow

BACK IN THE WINTER of the Blue Snow, the boys were logging the giant pines of the North Woods. It was a pretty big camp in those days, with a crew of 180 men. And every man was at least seven feet tall and weighed at least 350 pounds.

Joe Muffreau was too small to be a logger, being only six feet fourteen inches tall and weighing only 349 pounds and 53 ounces. But he was the fastest flapjack flipper in the North Woods, so they made him the camp cook.

One night, Joe looked out the window of the cookshack and saw something moving in the darkness. At first he thought it was a couple of pine trees coming in for dinner. But when it got closer, he realized it was a man—a big, big man with a bushy black beard, a red woolen cap, a plaid woolen shirt, and leather boots that were just about as tall as Joe Muffreau. Joe opened the door of the cookshack and smiled up at the stranger.

"You look mighty hungry," said Joe.

"I am," said the stranger. "My name's Paul Bunyan."

"Well, come on in and grab some grub."

Joe had a crew of twenty-two cookeys, and he put them all to work preparing dinner for the big lumberjack. After about three hours, it was all ready and Paul sat down to have himself a little meal. He ate thirty-three pounds of beef, one whole venison, six hams, two bushels of fried potatoes, twelve four-pound loaves of bread, twelve dozen eggs, and 678 flapjacks topped off with six gallons of maple syrup, and he washed it all down with twenty-two gallons of coffee.

When he was finished Paul said, "That'll tide me over. Now what about my ox?"

Joe looked out the window of the cookshack and squinted into the darkness. "What ox?" he asked. "All I see is a mountain covered with blue snow."

"That's no mountain—that's my ox," said Paul. "I call him Babe."

Joe looked out the window again. Sure enough, the mountain was really Babe, the Big Blue Ox. It was a reasonable mistake, because Babe was pretty big. Some folks say he measured fourteen ax handles between the eyes. Others say he measured forty-two and a half ax handles and a can of chewing tobacco. That just shows how people exaggerate. The truth is, Babe measured exactly seven ax handles between the eyes. . . . Of course, ax handles were a lot bigger in those days.

Joe had one of his boys show Paul and Babe to the stables. The stable boss let Babe eat as much as he wanted—which was a year's supply of hay for the entire camp. Then Paul and Babe knocked over a few hundred trees so they could lie down, and they went to sleep in the blue snow.

The next morning was crisp and clear and so cold that the thermometer outside Joe's cookshack froze at sixty below—it was perfect logging weather. After breakfast Paul and Babe went out with the lumberjacks to a section of tall pines. A section is a pretty big piece of land—640 acres—and the boys had been logging it all winter. It was slow, tedious work. Why, some of those North Woods pines were so big that a two-man team could saw at one side of the trunk for three days before they'd run into another team sawing from the other side.

Of course, Paul didn't work with a partner, and he didn't work with a saw. He stepped right up to the biggest tree he could find, lifted his giant ax, and chopped that North Woods pine down with a single stroke—*Boom!* The sound exploded like thunder in the cold air. Then he stepped over to another tree and did it again—*Boom!* The other loggers stared in wide-eyed wonder. The way Paul was going, they'd be done with the whole section by lunchtime.

Then Paul did something that really surprised them. He set his giant ax on the ground, scratched his bushy black beard, and said, "Boys, I don't mind working hard, but there's gotta be a better method of logging. This is just too slow. First we chop down the trees; then we pull them over the skid roads to the river. It seems like double work." Paul scratched his beard some more, and all the boys could see his cleverality working away in his big brain.

After a few minutes Paul got a light in his eyes. He picked up Babe's leather harness and wrapped it around the whole section—all 640 acres. Then the Big Blue Ox dragged the land, pine trees and all, down to the river. Paul and the boys cut the timber just like they were shearing a sheep, and the logs fell right into the river. Of course, the river was frozen at the time, but this way they were all set for the spring thaw. After the logs were cut, Babe hauled the section back where it belonged, and Paul hitched him up to another one.

With Paul and Babe, the Winter of the Blue Snow turned out to be the biggest logging season in the history of the world. When the spring thaw came, there were one hundred million logs in the river. Paul and the boys floated them down nice and easy at first, but the snow kept melting, the river kept getting higher, the logs kept moving faster, and pretty soon it was out of control. Those hundred million logs started bumping and stopping and sliding and piling, and all of a sudden Paul and the boys had a logjam to beat all jams. The logs were piled two hundred feet high and backed up a mile upriver.

Paul stood on the bank, scratching his bushy black beard. The boys could see his cleverality working pretty good. Finally Paul put Babe in the river and grabbed a shotgun. Then he peppered the Big Blue Ox with moose shot. Now, moose shot is good-sized ammunition, but Babe thought it was just a swarm of flies. He started swishing his tail around, stirring that river and stirring it some more, until pretty soon the whole dang river flowed backward and the logs came loose. Then Paul lifted Babe out of the water, and the logs floated downstream again.

Everything went pretty smoothly after that—until they got the logs to the sawmill. You see, Paul and the boys had so many logs, there weren't enough sawmills in the North Woods to buy them. Paul did a little checkin' around and discovered there was a big sawmill operator down near the Gulf of Mexico who was willing to buy all the logs they had. So the lumberjacks floated fifty million logs down the Mississippi River.

When the logs reached the Gulf of Mexico, the big sawmill operator refused to pay for them. Maybe he figured he was so far from the North Woods that he didn't have to worry about Paul Bunyan and the boys. But that's not the way Paul saw it. Paul never cared much about money—just logging—but a deal is a deal, and that fellow down on the Gulf of Mexico was cheating all the boys—and Babe, too. So Paul started scratching his beard and working his cleverality again. Then he got that light in his eyes, and the boys knew he had a plan.

Paul turned to Joe Muffreau and said, "Joe, I want you to bring me the biggest block of salt you can find."

"What about pepper?" asked Joe.

"No pepper," said Paul. "Just salt."

Joe sent his twenty-two cookeys back to the camp in an eight-horse flapjack wagon. When they came back, they were carrying a block of salt that was almost as big as Joe's cookshack. Paul picked it up in one hand and set it down in front of Babe, the Big Blue Ox. Well, Babe was always partial to salt, so he licked it and licked it until there was nothing left.

Of course, then Babe was pretty thirsty, so Paul led him over to the Mississippi River. Babe started drinking, and it must have tasted mighty good after that salt because he just kept drinking and drinking until the water came all the way up from the Gulf of Mexico with the fifty-million logs floating on the top.

Well, the sawmill operator paid right up after that. So Paul told Babe to stop drinking, and the Mississippi River flowed back down to the Gulf of Mexico, carrying the logs right with it. Paul split the profits with all the boys, including Babe. And that's what happened during the Winter of the Blue Snow.

No one knows how or when the tales of Paul Bunyan began. However, the lumberjacks of the North Woods were probably talking about

Paul Bunyan by the end of the nineteenth century. The first written story about Paul Bunyan was "The Round-River Drive," which appeared in a Detroit newspaper in 1910. These early stories were simpler and more realistic than later tales.

In 1914 a public relations man named W. B. Laughead began to use Paul Bunyan in an advertising campaign for the Red River Lumber Company of Westwood, California. Laughead wrote a series of advertising pamphlets in which he told many Paul Bunyan stories. He had heard some of these tales in the lumber camps, but he also made up many stories and characters, including Babe, the Big Blue Ox.

W. B. Laughead's advertising pamphlets made Paul Bunyan famous. Other writers began to retell old stories and make up new ones. Some of these stories moved Paul Bunyan away from the woods and into other activities, such as oil drilling and farming.

This tall tale is based on a number of early Paul Bunyan anecdotes. The meeting between Paul and Joe Muffreau was described by a lumberman named Fred Chaperon and recorded by Earl Clifton Beck in Songs of the Michigan Lumberjacks. *The story of Paul and Babe breaking up the log jam was recorded by K. Bernice Stewart and Homer A. Watt in "Legends of Paul Bunyan, Lumberjack." The other anecdotes are drawn from the pamphlets of W. B. Laughead as summarized by Daniel Hoffman in* Paul Bunyan: Last of the Frontier Demigods.

John Henry
Races the Steam Drill

THE BIG BEND TUNNEL WAS the longest tunnel in America—a mile and a quarter through the heart of the West Virginia mountains. The C & O Railroad started building it back around 1870. There was plenty of hard work for everyone, but the steel-driving men worked the hardest. And the hardest-working steel-driving man of them all was John Henry.

Now, John Henry was a powerful man—six feet tall and two hundred pounds of rippling muscle. He swung his nine-pound hammer from sunup to sundown, driving a steel drill into solid rock. Little Bill, the shaker, turned John Henry's drill between hammer blows and pulled it out when the hole was done. When there were enough holes, the demolition boys filled them with nitroglycerine and blew the rock to kingdom come. Then John Henry drove more steel—day after day in the heat and darkness and stale air of the tunnel.

John Henry always sang while he drove the steel—and at the end

of every line he brought that nine-pound hammer down like a crash of thunder.

This old hammer (Bam!)
Rings like silver (Bam!)
Shines like gold, boys, (Bam!)
Shines like gold. (Bam!)

Ain't no hammer (Bam!)
In these mountains (Bam!)
Rings like mine, boys, (Bam!)
Rings like mine. (Bam!)

One day, Captain Tommy interrupted John Henry in the middle of his song. "John Henry," he said, "the company wants to test one of those new steam drills. They say a steam drill can do the work of three or four men. But I say a good man can beat the steam. And I say you are the best man I have."

John Henry rested his nine-pound hammer on his broad, muscular shoulder. "Captain Tommy," he said, "a man ain't nothin' but a man. Before I let that steam drill beat me down, I'll die with my hammer in my hand."

"Son," offered Captain Tommy, "if you beat that steam drill, I'll give you one hundred dollars and a new suit of clothes."

"That's mighty generous," said John Henry, "but don't you worry about that. Just go to town and buy me a twenty-pound hammer. This nine-pound maul is feeling light."

The news of the contest spread through the camp like a strong wind whipping down the mountain. The company men said John

Henry was a poor working fool who didn't stand a chance against that mighty steam drill. Some of the working men thought the same. But the steel-driving men knew John Henry—and they believed in the power of a mighty man.

That night, John Henry told his wife, Polly Ann, about the contest. "Don't you strain yourself, honey," said Polly Ann. "'Course we could use that hundred dollars—and you need a new suit of clothes."

John Henry smiled and kissed Polly Ann. "I ain't worried about money or clothes," he said. "Don't y'see, sugar—a man ain't nothin' but a man, and a man got to beat the steam."

The next morning, the steel drivers crowded into the Big Bend Tunnel. It was hot and dusty, and the air was so foul that a man could hardly breathe. The only light was the flickering of lamps burning lard oil and blackstrap molasses.

The company man wheeled the steam drill into the tunnel and set it up against the rock. It was nothing but a machine—all shiny and modern and strange. Then John Henry walked in and stood beside it. He was nothing but a man—all black and fine and natural.

Captain Tommy handed John Henry a brand-new twenty-pound hammer. "There ain't another like it in West Virginia," he said. "Good luck, son."

John Henry held the hammer in his hand and felt its fine natural weight. In the flickering light of the tunnel, the head of that hammer shone like gold. "Gonna call this hammer Polly Ann," he said.

Little Bill sat on the rock, holding the six-foot drill in his hands. John Henry towered above the steel, just waiting to begin. It was so quiet in that tunnel, you could hear the soft breathing of the steel-driving men.

Captain Tommy blew his whistle. The company man turned on

the steam drill. John Henry swung his twenty-pound hammer back and brought it down with a crash like thunder. As he swung it back again he began to sing:

> *This old hammer* (Bam!)
> *Rings like silver* (Bam!)
> *Shines like gold, boys,* (Bam!)
> *Shines like gold.* (Bam!)

John Henry kept driving steel and the steam drill kept drilling. Pretty soon the whole mountain was rumbling and shaking. John Henry's muscles bulged and strained like they never bulged and strained before. Sweat cascaded down his powerful chest, and veins protruded from the sides of his handsome face.

"Are you all right, John Henry?" asked Captain Tommy.

"Don't you worry," said John Henry. "A man ain't nothin' but a man—and a man got to beat the steam." Then he went on singing:

Ain't no hammer (Bam!)
In these mountains (Bam!)
Rings like mine, boys, (Bam!)
Rings like mine. (Bam!)

When they hit the end of the six-foot drill, Little Bill pulled it out and shoved in a longer drill—and then a longer one and a longer one still. John Henry swung his twenty-pound hammer and drove that steel. He swung and drove faster and harder, and faster and harder, until that Polly Ann hammer caught fire. The whole Big Bend tunnel glowed with the blue flame of John Henry's hammer.

"Time!" shouted Captain Tommy.

"Time!" cried the company man, shutting off the steam drill.

"Time," gasped John Henry, leaning on his hammer. "I need a cool drink of water."

While John Henry drank his water, Captain Tommy and the company man measured the holes. The steam drill had done nine feet; John Henry had drilled fourteen.

"John Henry!" shouted the steel drivers. "John Henry beat the steam!"

"Congratulations, son," said Captain Tommy, slapping him on the back. "I don't care what you say—I'm gonna give you a hundred dollars and a new suit of clothes."

John Henry leaned heavily on his hammer and sucked in the stale air of the tunnel. "That's mighty generous, Captain Tommy. But you give that hundred dollars to Polly Ann. And you bury me in that suit of clothes." Then he slumped to the ground, clutching his hammer in his hand. "I beat the steam," he gasped, "but I broke inside."

As his eyes closed, John Henry lay back against the black earth and whispered, "A man ain't nothin' but a man."

———

No one knows the true story of John Henry. However, some folklore experts believe that there was a great steel driver named John Henry, who had a contest with a steam drill in the Big Bend Tunnel in 1870. The real John Henry probably did not die immediately after the contest but rather in one of the many accidents that were common in early tunnel construction. Shortly afterward, the story of John Henry was told in two kinds of songs: hammer songs, like the one that John Henry sings in this tale, and ballads, which are longer and tell more of the story. By the late 1920s, when folklore experts began to study the John Henry legend seriously, there were more than one hundred hammer songs and one hundred versions of the ballad. This tall tale is based on several different ballads collected by Louis W. Chappel in John Henry: A Folk-Lore Study *and by Guy Johnson in* John Henry: Tracking Down a Negro Legend.

Gib Morgan

Brings in the Well

GIB MORGAN WAS THE BEST driller in the oil business. He wasn't much to look at—just a skinny little man in baggy pants and a gray slouch hat—but he had a brain as big as Texas, and maybe a little bit of Oklahoma, too. If there was oil, Gib was sure to find it. Gib Morgan always brought in the well.

There was one time, though, when Gib almost came up dry. It was a well down in east Texas. The rockhounds—some folks call them petroleum engineers—were positive there was oil, but the digging crew couldn't dig a hole deep enough to reach it. Every time they got close to the oil, the ground caved in and filled up the well. Then they had to start all over again.

Finally Gib took over the job. First he ordered some special drilling tools—very, very big ones and very, very small ones and all the sizes in between. While the tools were being made, he went down to Texas to build the derrick—that's the structure that holds the cable and the

drilling tools. Gib knew he needed something on the large side, so he built a derrick that covered an acre of ground and reached so high it practically disappeared in the Texas sky.

That evening Gib took a little rest about a hundred feet down from the top of the derrick. He lay back against a girder, tilted his gray slouch hat over his forehead, and watched the moon rising over the oil field. Suddenly he realized the derrick was so doggone tall, the moon was gonna bump right into it! Gib scrambled up the derrick and slapped a hinge on the last fifty feet so he could fold the top down to let the moon pass by.

Gib's derrick was so tall that it took the average man fourteen days to climb to the top. So he had to hire thirty tool dressers to help him. On any given day, there was one tool dresser greasing the crown pulleys on top of the derrick, one tool dresser sharpening the drill bits at the bottom, and twenty-eight tool dressers climbing up or down. Gib built bunkhouses along the way with hot and cold showers and all the modern conveniences.

When the special tools arrived, the tool dressers manned their stations and Gib commenced to drill. His first drill bit was about one-hundred feet in diameter. He went down a little ways with that one, but the ground started caving in. So he took a million-gallon oil tank—with the top and bottom cut out—and set it into the hole to keep it from collapsing. Then he put on a smaller drill bit—ninety feet in diameter. He went down a little farther, and the ground started caving in again. So he set an 850-thousand-gallon oil tank into the hole and put on a smaller drill bit.

Well, this went on for a month or so, with Gib using smaller and smaller drill bits every few hours. In the meantime, the thirty tool dressers were climbing up and down the derrick, and of course every night one of them had to fold the derrick to let the moon pass by.

Now, Gib was a great one for concentration, but all this climbing up and down—not to mention the collapsing ground—was starting to drive him a little crazy. Then one day as he was changing a drill bit, he heard a deep voice behind him. "Mr. Morgan," said the voice, "can you use another tool dresser?"

Gib figured he could always use another tool dresser, so he turned around to take a look at the fellow. All he could see was a big pair of boots. Gib craned his neck out of the derrick and followed the rest of the fellow all the way up to the Texas sky. He was the biggest tool dresser Gib had ever seen.

"What's your name?" Gib asked.

"Big Toolie," he answered.

"Do me a little favor," said Gib. "See if you can reach the crown pulleys on top of the derrick."

Big Toolie did as he was told. It was a bit of a stretch, but he could touch the crown pulleys with his boots on the ground.

"Tell you what," said Gib. "Pick those little fellows off the derrick and get to work. We got a well to drill."

With Big Toolie greasing the crown pulleys and sharpening the bits, Gib could concentrate on the drilling. Things went smoothly for a while, and the well kept getting deeper and narrower. Whenever he felt the ground caving in, Gib supported the sides with a casing and switched to a smaller bit. Pretty soon, he was using bits that weren't much thicker than his fingers. That's when he ran out of drilling cable.

"Gol' durn it!" Gib exclaimed. "I can feel that black oil down there just waitin' for me to find it."

"Whatcha gonna do, boss?" Big Toolie asked.

Gib tilted his gray slouch hat back on his head and set his brain to working. "Well," he said, "I could send for more cable. But that blasted well is so deep and narrow that it's just gonna fill up with sand every time I drill. Nope, this is a job for Strickie."

"Strickie, boss?"

"Yep," said Gib. "He's the longest, smartest, best-natured boa constrictor I ever knew. Met him when I was drilling in the jungle of Brazil. Of course, he's retired now, living in a rooming house in Brooklyn. But I think I can persuade him to help us."

Gib sent Strickie an urgent telegram and one hundred dollars expense money. As soon as he read the telegram, the big boa constrictor slithered across the Brooklyn Bridge and boarded the next train for Texas. He was so long, he had to rent two whole sleeping cars, and the engineer set a railroad speed record just to get him off the train. Pretty soon Gib and Strickie were reunited in the oil field.

"Strickie," said Gib, "it sure is good to see you and I'd love to talk over old times in the jungle, but we got work to do."

Strickie nodded his head and let Gib tie his tail to the end of the drilling cable. Then the boa constrictor slithered right down the well and headed for the bottom. When he hit the sand, he just opened his jaws and started eating his way down toward the oil. It didn't matter if the sides collapsed, because he just ate the collapsing ground. He was like a drill bit, a cable, and a casing all rolled into one.

With Strickie in the well and Big Toolie greasing the crown pulleys, Gib figured that oil was practically his. But all of a sudden he felt three long tugs on the cable. It was Strickie's signal that he wanted to come up to the surface. So Gib hauled him out of the well, and he could see the problem right away: Strickie was stretched out so long

66

and tight that his scales were about to pop off. It was obvious that he couldn't stretch another inch.

"Dang it!" Gib exclaimed. "That's the deepest, strongest well I ever drilled—five thousand feet and I still haven't hit oil. But it's down there and it's close, real close. I can smell it."

"Whatcha gonna do, boss?" asked Big Toolie.

"I don't know," said Gib, "but I've never met a well I couldn't drill."

Gib sat on his stool, tilted his slouch hat down on his forehead, and considered the situation. He considered and considered some more. There wasn't a man in the oil business who could consider like Gib Morgan. Finally he came up with an idea.

Gib reached into his tool kit and found a needle, a thread, and a straw. He looped one end of the thread through the eye of the needle, tied the other end around Strickie's lower jaw, and put the straw into the snake's mouth. He could tell by the light in Strickie's eyes that the boa constrictor knew exactly what he had in mind. That snake was mighty smart.

Gib lowered Strickie back into the well, through the million-gallon oil tank and the 850-thousand-gallon tank and all the rest of the tanks and casings until finally he hit the bottom. The big boa stretched as far as he could stretch, pushed the straw into the sand, and sucked the hole clean. Then he dropped the needle and thread through the straw.

There was a loud hissing and the sweet smell of natural gas. Gib and Big Toolie hauled Strickie back to the surface like greased lightning. Then it came: the beautiful black explosion of oil, gushing out through the top of the well—past Gib Morgan, past Strickie, past Big Toolie, past the top of the giant derrick, and into the clear blue Texas sky. It was the biggest, richest gusher in the history of the oil business—and Gib Morgan brought it in with a needle and thread.

Gib Morgan was born in 1842 in western Pennsylvania, the site of the early American oil industry. After serving in the Civil War, Gib worked as a driller and tool dresser in Pennsylvania, West Virginia, and Ohio. During his life in the oil fields, Morgan made up over fifty humorous tales with himself as the hero, always emphasizing his intelligence and creativity rather than his strength. Many of the tales were set in places he had never visited—Texas, South America, and the Fiji Islands.

By the time of his death in 1909, Gib Morgan and his stories were famous throughout the oil industry. Many Gib Morgan stories were later retold about Paul Bunyan. This tall tale is based on several stories recorded by Mody C. Boatright in Gib Morgan, Minstrel of the Oil Fields.

Pecos Bill Finds a Ranch
but Loses a Wife

PECOS BILL WAS A FULL-FLEDGED cowboy at the age most folks are learning to tie their shoes. Of course Bill didn't wear shoes—he wore boots, a big Stetson hat, a red bandanna, and chaps that carried half the dust in west Texas. They called him Pecos Bill because he got bounced out of the family wagon when he was just a baby and landed right smack dab in the middle of the Pecos River.

When Bill first showed up on the range, cowboys were kind of primitive—they just rode around the cows yelping and howling. Then Bill invented a few useful tools like the six-shooter, the lariat, and the branding iron. He also invented stagecoach robbing, but he never took it seriously.

More than anything, Bill wanted to start a ranch of his own. Most of the land in Texas was fenced in and spoken for, so he rode west into what we call New Mexico today. Bill thought it was just about the nicest-looking piece of real estate he ever saw. He staked out the whole

state for a ranch and fenced in Arizona for a calf pasture. Now all he needed was a few good men to work the ranch. He was riding around aimlessly when he ran into an old prospector.

"Tell me, old-timer," he asked, "have you seen any likely looking cowhands in these parts? I mean *real* cowhands—the kind that eat beans for dinner, swallow prairie dogs for dessert, and use barbed wire to pick their teeth?"

The old prospector took one look at Bill and saw that he wasn't your ordinary behind-the-desk kind of rancher. "Sure thing, young feller," he said. "There's a bunch of rough customers camping out about two hundred miles down this here wash. But I gotta warn you—they're tough hombres."

"That's what I'm looking for," said Bill. He rode down the wash feeling pretty optimistic. But after a hundred miles or so, his horse got spooked by something on the trail. It reared up on its hind legs, and Bill held onto the saddle horn for all he was worth. The doggone cinch broke, and the saddle slipped right down the horse's back, taking Bill with it. The horse ran back up the wash, leaving Bill all alone in the middle of the trail with nothing but a saddle.

Well, Bill was feeling pretty ornery to begin with, but he got downright peevish when he saw what had spooked his horse. There was a ten-foot rattlesnake coiled up in his path, just shaking those rattles and asking for a fight. Bill set his saddle down and—just to be fair—gave the rattler the first three bites. Then he started beating the poison out of that big rattlesnake until the poor miserable reptile begged for mercy.

"Please, Bill," said the rattler, "I was just fooling around. I wasn't looking for a real fight."

"You ain't seen a real fight," said Bill. He picked up the snake,

71

slung his saddle over his shoulder, and walked on down the wash, twirling the rattlesnake like a lariat and looping a few Gila monsters just to pass the time.

After about forty miles or so, a mountain lion jumped down from a cliff and landed right on Bill's neck, biting away with all the strength it could muster. It was a good-sized mountain lion, too—a little bigger than three steers and a calf.

Bill chuckled to himself and set his saddle and snake on the ground. Then he lit into that mountain lion until the fur was flying so thick that it blocked the sun up and down the wash. In about two and a half minutes the mountain lion got down on its knees and apologized. "Sorry, Bill," said the lion. "Can't you take a joke?"

"I can take a joke," Bill replied. "What I can't take is walking." So Bill set his saddle on the back of the mountain lion and tied the cinch good and tight. Then he picked up the rattlesnake and rode on down the wash, whooping and hollering and having a good old time. Things went a little faster after that, with Bill using the rattlesnake for a whip and riding that big mountain lion a hundred feet at a step.

When he found the camp of the tough hombres, Bill rode right up to the chuck wagon, twirling his rattler and letting loose with a couple of bloodcurdling war whoops. He jerked back on the mountain lion, climbed on down, and hung the snake around his neck. Then he grabbed ten or twenty handfuls of hot beans, swallowed a few prairie dogs, and washed it all down with a couple gallons of boiling coffee. When he was full, he wiped his face on a prickly pear cactus.

"Who's the boss around here?" he asked.

A tough-looking, eight-foot, 300-pound hombre with pistols and bullets and bowie knives strapped all over his chest walked up to Bill kind of meek and polite and careful. "I was," he said, "but I ain't about to argue with a man who rides a mountain lion, twirls a rattle-snake, and uses a cactus for a napkin. You're the boss, now—boss."

Bill nodded at the giant hombre and took a look at the men. They were a rough, tough-looking bunch, sitting around the campfire and picking their teeth with barbed wire. That old prospector was right—they were just the men he needed. Twirling his ten-foot rattlesnake, Bill hopped on the back of his mountain lion and waved his hat in the air. "C'mon, boys!" he roared. "I got a little ranch I call New Mexico."

With his new cowhands, Bill had the ranch working in no time. He put the giant hombre in charge of the cattle, and he looked after the horses himself. One little colt really caught Bill's eye. He was pure black and full of fire from the minute he stood on four legs. Bill named him Widow-Maker, and he raised him on nitroglycerine and dynamite. Normally Bill wouldn't let other people near Widow-Maker—for their own safety, of course. But he made one exception, and he never forgave himself.

You see, Bill was always popular with the ladies, but he only fell in love once. The gal's name was Slue-Foot Sue, and Bill first saw her riding a catfish on the Rio Grande. In those days, Rio Grande catfish were about as big as whales, so you can imagine that Bill was mighty love struck. Sue was just as moony over Bill, so they decided to get married as soon as she could get herself a proper wedding dress.

Of course, back then all the ladies' dresses had big steel-spring bustles in the behind. When Sue's dress arrived it had the biggest bustle a dress could have. She slipped right into the contraption, and Bill dusted off his chaps. The wedding was the rip-roaringest party west of the Pecos River. In the middle of all the whooping and cele-brating, Sue turned to Bill and asked, "Honey, can I ride your horse?"

"Now, darling," said Bill, "you know I don't let anyone ride Widow-Maker."

"But you've seen me ride the catfish," answered Sue. "And besides, I'm your wife. What's yours is mine and what's mine is yours."

Well, Slue-Foot Sue was such a beautiful bride that Bill's tough old heart got kinda soft and mushy. "Okay," he said. "Just this once."

Sue ran right over to Widow-Maker and hopped on, wedding dress and all. Widow-Maker flashed Bill a what-do-you-think-you're-doing kind of look. He started to buck and bronc and buck some more. Anyone else would've been thrown with the first few bucks, but Slue-Foot Sue was an expert rider and she hung on tight. That got Widow-Maker even angrier, so he bucked and broncked again. But this time it was serious bucking and broncking. The ground shook and cracked all the way down to the Rio Grande, and Widow-Maker threw Slue-Foot Sue so high she had to duck to avoid hitting her head on the moon.

When Sue ran out of up-speed she started coming down faster and faster until she was streaking like a comet. She hit the ground, bounced on that big steel-spring bustle of hers, and went flying up again, higher than before. About a half hour later, she came down and bounced again, flying even higher. This went on and on, with Sue gaining altitude after every bounce.

Bill stood all mopey and sorrowful, watching his bouncing bride and feeling completely helpless. He considered shooting her to put her out of her misery, but he just didn't have the heart. He watched for a couple of weeks, until the bounces started coming every other day. Then he mounted Widow-Maker and rode away. Most folks think Slue-Foot Sue is still bouncing somewhere up around Jupiter.

Bill never really recovered from the loss of Slue-Foot Sue. He always had a sorrowful expression on his face, and he just plain refused to laugh. The truth is, old Pecos Bill was pretty darn miserable.

Then, one day, he met a fella from back East who was wearing a mail-order cowboy suit with shiny spangles and nice clean chaps that never saw a speck of range dust. The eastern dude cornered Bill and started asking him ridiculous questions about the West, like "Where's Texas?" and "Do rattlesnakes really rattle?"

At first Bill tried to be polite and answer the fella's questions as if they were almost reasonable. But after about forty-seven questions the eastern dude tipped back his mail-order cowboy hat, pushed out his shiny spangled chest, and said, "Yep, I guess I'm a real cowboy now."

That was too much. Bill smiled a little and then he smiled a little more. And then he laughed—and laughed some more. He laughed a little harder and harder still, until pretty soon he was laughing so hard he could barely breathe. Finally, he just lay down in the dust of New Mexico and plain laughed himself to death.

From the earliest days of riding the range, cowboys told tall tales around the campfire. The hero of these tales was usually a local cowboy or the storyteller himself. It was only in the early twentieth century that Pecos Bill became a tall tale hero.

The first written story was "The Saga of Pecos Bill," by Edward O'Reilly, published in the Century Magazine *in 1923. Some folklore experts believe that O'Reilly made the story up completely, while others think he heard some of the anecdotes from old cowboys. After the appearance of O'Reilly's story, other writers wrote Pecos Bill stories and cowboys adopted Pecos Bill as a genuine hero. This tall tale is based on O'Reilly's original story.*

Annotated Bibliography

Asbury, Herbert. *The Gangs of New York*, pp. 23–37. New York: Alfred A. Knopf, 1928. Discusses Big Mose and the Bowery.

———. *Ye Olde Fire Laddies,* pp. 152–84. New York: Alfred A. Knopf, 1930. Discusses Big Mose, Moses Humphrey, and the early New York City Fire Department.

Baker, Benjamin A. *A Glance at New York.* New York: Samuel French, 1848. The original Mose play.

Beck, Earl Clifton, ed. "Paul's Dinner." *Songs of the Michigan Lumberjacks.* Ann Arbor: University of Michigan Press, 1941. Reprinted in Felton, pp. 32–36. Oral tale of Paul's meeting with Joe Muffreau, the cook.

Boatright, Mody C. *Gib Morgan, Minstrel of the Oil Fields.* Texas Folklore Society publication no. XX. Dallas: Southern Methodist University Press, 1965. Contains fifty-one stories told by Gib Morgan, introduced by a biographical essay.

Botkin, B. A., ed. *A Treasury of American Folklore.* New York: Crown, 1944. Reprint. New York: Bonanza Books, 1983. Probably the best anthology, but does not separate earlier, more authentic tales from later versions; reprints many early sources that are difficult to find.

Chappel, Louis W. *John Henry: A Folk-Lore Study.* Jena, Germany: Frommer, 1933. Reprint. Port Washington, NY: Kennikat Press, 1968. Scholarly study of the John Henry legend; contains thirty variations of the ballad and five variations of the hammer song; most are different from those collected by Johnson.

Chittenden, Hiram Martin. *The Yellowstone National Park*, pp. 51–57. Cincinnati: The Robert Clarke Company, 1895. Includes biographical information along with the tales; written by a man who knew Bridger.

Dorson, Richard Mercer, ed. *Davy Crockett, American Comic Legend.* New York: Rockland Editions, 1939. Reprint. Westport, CT: Greenwood Press, 1977. Contains 108 selections from the *Crockett Almanacs* of 1835–1856, with an introductory essay by one of America's greatest experts on folklore.

Felton, Harold W., ed. *Legends of Paul Bunyan.* New York: Alfred A. Knopf, 1947. Popular anthology that makes no attempt to separate earlier authentic tales from later stories by commercial writers; includes some early sources that are difficult to find.

Hoffman, Daniel. *Paul Bunyan: Last of the Frontier Demigods*, pp. 73–83. Philadelphia: Temple University, 1952. Excellent critical discussion of the Paul Bunyan legend, including a summary of ideas from W. B. Laughead's advertising pamphlets; the original pamphlets are very difficult to find.

Jagendorf, Moritz. *The Marvelous Adventures of Johnny Caesar Cicero Darling*. New York: Vanguard Press, 1949. Contains stories told by people of the Catskills, many of whom heard them originally from John Darling.

Johnson, Guy. *John Henry: Tracking Down a Negro Legend*. Chapel Hill: University of North Carolina Press, 1929. Scholarly study of the John Henry legend; contains thirty variations of the ballad and eleven variations of the hammer song; most are different from those collected by Chappel.

O'Reilly, Edward. "The Saga of Pecos Bill." *Century Magazine* 106 (no. 6, October 1923), pp. 827–833. Reprinted in Botkin, pp. 180–85. The original written version of the Pecos Bill tales.

Shay, Frank. *Here's Audacity! American Legendary Folk Heroes*, pp. 17–30. New York: The Macaulay Company, 1930. The original written version of the Old Stormalong tales.

———. *American Sea Songs and Chanteys from the Days of Iron Men and Wooden Ships*, pp. 63–65. Freeport, NY: Books For Libraries Press, 1969. Originally published 1924 as *Iron Men and Wooden Ships*. A collection of nineteenth-century sailing songs.

Stewart, K. Bernice, and Homer A. Watt. "Legends of Paul Bunyan, Lumberjack." *Transactions of the Wisconsin Academy of Sciences, Arts, and Letters* XVIII, part ii, pp. 639–51, 1916. Reprinted in Felton, p. 101. First written record of the big log jam story.

The illustrations in this book were done in gouache
and Prismacolor pencil on BFK paper.
The display type was set in Centaur.
The text type was set in Bembo.
Composition by Thompson Type, San Diego, California
Color separations by Bright Arts, Ltd., Singapore
Printed and bound by Tien Wah Press, Singapore
Production supervision by Warren Wallerstein and David Hough
Designed by Trina Stahl